JONATHAN MICHAEL

AND

MOTHER NATURE'S FURY

By CYNDI HARPER-DEITERS

Illustrated by HELEN M. BOWERS

To: Wayne

Enjoy Nature!

Cyndi Harper-Deiters

10-23-93

Helen M. Bowers

Country Home Publishers   Fremont, MI 49412

ACKNOWLEDGEMENTS

Robert Ruggles and Grace Ruggles
For their hours of editing and proofreading.

Other books by this author:
JONATHAN MICHAEL THE RESIDENT ROOSTER
JONATHAN MICHAEL AND THE UNINVITED GUEST

This series is designed to encourage its audience
to problem solve without the use of physical violence.

Dear Mother and Mother-in-Law,
Thank you for the prayers
that carry me through
life's storms.

Jonathan Michael sighed while lying in the hay mound staring out at the night's beauty. He carefully read the evening's weather map. The halo around the moon shared its wisdom of tomorrow's rain. The cluster of stars dazzling the gray, overcast sky confirmed the sunset's announcement of showers coming with the next sunrise.

Jonathan Michael knew that this would disappoint Farmer Troyer, because the corn needed to be planted soon. The freshly dug earth's musky scent filled the air. The heavy plow was pulled behind Nora and Martha earlier today, opening the earth, so seeds could be planted into it.

Just before dawn Jonathan Michael rose and wandered across the barnyard. With a quick upward hop with his feet and a flap of his wings, he flew up to his favorite fence-post. The red sunrise showed no mercy in its prediction of the day's weather. It whispered, "rain is coming," as wispy clouds danced across its pale-melon glow.

Jonathan Michael announced the new day with his re-sounding "COCKA-DOODLE-DOO!"

Then he sped away toward the barnyard to make his morning inspections before breakfast.

5

Hearing some loud cackling outside the hen house, Jonathan Michael went in that direction and peeked around the corner. Standing with his beak hanging toward the ground is Helmer, Daisy May's rooster-chick that hatched this spring. Jonathan Michael could overhear Daisy May scolding him for running off and exploring without permission and then not answering her calls for him to come back. He turned to walk away when he heard his name being called. He looked back and saw Helmer coming up behind him. "May I go with you on morning inspections, Jonathan Michael?" Helmer asked.

Jonathan Michael looked over to Daisy May who nodded with approval. "Yes, you may join me, Helmer," he said. In step with each other they headed toward the barn.

Marybell, Buttercup, and Blossom were already stand-ing in the milk stanchions. Farmer Troyer passed Jonathan Michael and Helmer mumbling that the cows didn't give much milk this morning. Jonathan Michael knew that the lack of milk was a good sign that it was going to be a stormy day.

After saying his good mornings to the cows, Jonathan Michael, with Helmer beside him, went to the other side of the barn.

Nora and Martha were still in their stalls chewing on some grain. "Good morning, Jonathan Michael. Who is your little friend?" Nora asked.

"Ladies, I would like to introduce Helmer. He is one of Daisy May's spring chicks," Jonathan Michael replied.

"How do you do," Helmer said while bowing gracefully.

"What a little gentleman he is," Nora and Martha laughed.

"I don't think we will be planting that corn today," Martha announced while stretching out her neck and sniffing the rain in the air.

"No, it doesn't look good out there this morning," Jonathan Michael agreed while moving away from the stall.

"Good morning, Jonathan Michael and little fellow," Hank neighed out to them as they approached his and Henry's stable.

Reaching the horses, Jonathan Michael noticed that their coats were wet from sweat. "Have you been out already this morning?" Jonathan Michael asked.

"No, just been eating some hay," Henry answered.

"Good thing it is Saturday, because it sure feels like rain today," Hank said.

"It's good there is no school today. I also noticed that the clover leaves were closed on the way over this morning. Surely a storm is brewing," Jonathan Michael said. "Well, I have to be on my way. I'll see you later," Jonathan Michael called, turning to leave.

"Good morning, Tressie and Bessie," Jonathan Michael said while hopping up on the fence post, forgetting Helmer was too small to join him there.

"Good morning," they muffled while holding hay in their mouths.

"I see you are preparing for a rainy day. Where are your piglets this morning?" Jonathan Michael asked.

"They are in the hut where they will stay dry and warm. We have been taking the extra hay in there for all of us. You know that there is a storm coming this way, don't you?" Tressie asked.

"Yes, I have been noticing signs of a rain storm this morning," Jonathan Michael replied. "I'll check on you later," he said, hopping off the fence and motioning for Helmer to follow him.

Jonathan Michael went back to the hen house to return Helmer. The hens were running around acting frightened, because they, too, knew a storm was coming.

"Gather up your chicks and go inside the hen house for the day," Jonathan Michael suggested while gentle pushing Helmer with his wing tip toward Daisy May.

"Yes, we shall do that," they all cackled, swooping up their chicks.

17

Jonathan Michael went to the barn and began eating his breakfast. The heavy damp air made him feel sleepier than usual, so he went up into the hay mound to take a long nap. It wasn't long and he was fast asleep.

The howling wind and tree branches brushing up against the barn and Daisy May's screeching woke him up.

He quickly leaped from the hay mound and ran out of the barn in the direction of the hen house.

When he reached Daisy May, she was crying and upset. "What is wrong?" he asked.

"It is Helmer, he has run off again and I cannot find him, and it is getting so windy out here; I'm afraid that he will get caught in the storm!" she cried.

"Calm down now, Daisy May. I will go and find Helmer," Jonathan Michael said.

Jonathan Michael began his search for Helmer by going through the barn. None of the animals there had seen him, so he went out toward the other buildings.

The wind, now blowing from the east, lifted Jonathan Michael's feathers, causing him to shiver from the arrival of cooler air. The heavy, blackened clouds hung low to the earth. Rain was spilling from them, causing puddles to be formed quickly around his feet.

Jonathan Michael splashed through one puddle after another crossing the barnyard and checking in each building. Helmer was not in any of them.

21

With each step Jonathan Michael grew more concerned, because the storm was becoming more violent with each passing moment. Lightning was flashing brightly across the sky, and thunder was crashing and rumbling so loudly that it hurt his ears.

There were small pebbles of hailstones covering the ground and hitting Jonathan Michael as they dropped. His skin pricked with pain when some cut through his layers of feathers.

Jonathan Michael knew that he must find Helmer. If he were caught out in this storm he would not survive. Helmer was too small to have enough feathers to protect him from the rain and hail. The colder air and wicked winds would cause pneumonia.

"I must find him, his life depends on me!" Jonathan Michael cried into the storm.

Jonathan Michael's search had taken him far beyond the barnyard and, still, there was no sign of Helmer.

He was completely drenched now. His beautiful tail feathers dragging through the mud left a strange trail behind him on the soaked earth. With a painful, hoarse voice he again called into the raging storm's fury, "Helmer, where are you?"

The bright flash of lightning dancing across the black sky above the neighboring orchard was the only light he had to guide his way.

He pushed forward against the strong, wicked east wind. The trees in the orchard were swaying violently in the storm. Apple blossoms stripped from the branches flew helplessly with the wind. Branches were savagely ripped from the tree trunks and thrown around as if they were toothpicks. Apple crates were carried into the sky and then smashed into broken heaps of kindling on the ground.

Jonathan Michael feared that this was more than a spring thunder storm. Suddenly, the sound of church bells broke into the roaring storm's angry clamor and he knew that they were warning that a tornado had been sighted. He must find cover and he must find Helmer!

27

.His breath was sucked away from him as he lifted his head and looked into the sky, searching it for a funnel cloud. He could see nothing in the blackness surrounding him.

"Helmer, are you here?" he choked with a sore throat.

"Peep, peep, here I am," Helmer cried.

"Keep calling Helmer, so I can follow the sound of your voice," Jonathan Michael commanded.

"I'm here under an apple crate that blew over. Please hurry! I'm really scared!" Helmer called.

Jonathan Michael stood right in front of the crate that was holding Helmer prisoner when a flash of lightning lit the sky. Jonathan Michael could see two little eyes peeking out between the crate's slats at him. "Helmer, are you all right?" he asked.

"Yes, but I want to go home!" he cried.

Jonathan Michael pushed the crate over, releasing Helmer. "Quickly, Helmer, we must find cover!" Jonathan Michael yelled. With Helmer under one of his wings to protect him from the strong wind and the falling debris, Jonathan Michael pushed against the storm's fury.

At last he spotted the irrigation ditch that ran along side the orchard and they tumbled into it. "We will stay here until the storm has passed over," Jonathan Michael said, checking the water level around them. He knew they couldn't stay in the ditch long, because water was starting to rush into it.

The storm ended as abruptly as it had begun. The rain stopped and the wind shifted into a westerly breeze. Jonathan Michael looked up and marveled at the beautiful huge rainbow arched high above the barnyard with the sun's rays graciously shining through it.

Jonathan Michael lifted his wing and looked into Helmer's eyes saying, "The storm has passed. It is safe to come out now. We must get back to the barnyard and see how everybody is." With that, they raced across the orchard and through the muddy field toward the farm.

Reaching the barn, Jonathan Michael could see where some roof shingles had been torn from it. Tree branches were flung about and fence posts were tipped sideways, but all the buildings were still standing.

He first went to the hen house where the hens, all except Daisy May, were busy picking up worms that had washed to the surface. Daisy May was crying over Helmer when Jonathan Michael called out to her, "Helmer is all right. He is right here." Daisy May rushed over to them. Hugging Helmer close to her, she turned and thanked Jonathan Michael for bringing him back to her safely.

After making sure that all the hens were okay, Jonathan Michael rushed toward the barn to check on the others.

Tressie, Bessie, and the piglets were all squealing in delight while rolling in the mud left behind.

He met Marybell, Buttercup, and Blossom just as they were heading out to the pasture. "What a storm!" they said in passing.

35

Inside the barn, Hank and Henry were enjoying a visit with Nora and Martha. Jonathan Michael joined them. They all talked about the storm. They were fascinated when he told them about his and Helmer's experience.

With a big yawn, he bid them all good night. Ascending to the top of the hay mound, he could see the setting sun, casting red all around it, promising fair weather for tomorrow.

The hay smelled so sweet and felt so soft; he dropped into it exhausted. The rhythm of Farmer Troyer's hammer nailing new shingles on the roof relaxed him.

Sleep took over him while counting his blessings for the day and looking forward to those that would be added in future adventures with his barnyard friends.

GOOD NIGHT

37

ORDER YOUR COPY TODAY!

Send check or money order (U.S. Dollars only) to:
Country Home Publishers, Box 360, Fremont, MI 49412

Please send:

_____ copy(s) of JONATHAN MICHAEL THE RESIDENT ROOSTER

_____ copy(s) of JONATHAN MICHAEL AND THE UNINVITED GUEST

_____ copy(s) of JONATHAN MICHAEL AND MOTHER NATURE'S FURY

at $4.95 each plus $1.35 shipping and handling*

_____ please add me to the mailing list to be notified when the next book of the series is available

_____ order today a: COLORED JONATHAN MICHAEL WALL POSTER at $1.50 each plus $1.25 shipping and handling

I would like my book(s) autographed by author and addressed to:

_____

MI residents, add 4% sales tax.

Name _____

Address _____

City _____ State _____ Zip _____

*Shipping fees for more than one book:
Two-three books $1.85; four-five books $2.50; six or more books add 30¢ for each book.